Little Miss Muffet
and friends

Miles KeLLy

First published in 2011 by Miles Kelly Publishing Ltd
Harding's Barn, Bardfield End Green, Thaxted, Essex, CM6 3PX, UK

This edition published 2012 for Index Books

4 6 8 10 9 7 5

Publishing Director Belinda Gallagher
Creative Director Jo Cowan
Editor Sarah Parkin
Cover/Junior Designer Kayleigh Allen
Production Manager Elizabeth Collins
Reprographics Stephan Davis, Ian Paulyn
Assets Lorraine King

ISBN 978-1-84810-416-7

Printed in China

British Library Cataloguing-in-Publication Data
A catalogue record for this book is available from the British Library

ACKNOWLEDGEMENTS

Artworks are from the Miles Kelly Artwork Bank
Cover artist: Mike Phillips

Made with paper from a sustainable forest

www.mileskelly.net
info@mileskelly.net
www.factsforprojects.com

Contents

Two Little Dickie-birds

Two little dickie-birds,
Sitting on a wall,
One named Peter,
The other named Paul.

Fly away, Peter!
Fly away, Paul!
Come back, Peter!
Come back, Paul!

Use your index fingers to be Peter and Paul.

Wiggle each finger in turn.

Next, put each finger behind you as if to fly away.

On the last line, bring each finger back in front of you.

What does the Bee do?

What does the bee do?
What does the bee do?
Bring home honey.
And what does Father do?
Bring home money.
And what does Mother do?
Lay out the money.
And what does baby do?
Eat up the honey.

Christina Rossetti
1830–94, b. England

Lucy Locket

Lucy Locket lost her pocket,
Kitty Fisher found it;
There was not a penny in it,
But a ribbon round it.

Three Blind Mice

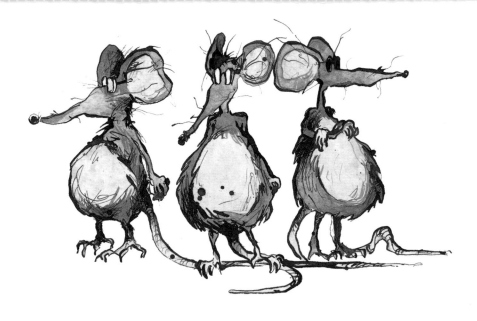

Three blind mice, three blind mice,
See how they run! See how they run!
They all ran after the farmer's wife,
Who cut off their tails with
a carving knife,
Did you ever see such a thing in your life,
As three blind mice?

The Elves and the Shoemaker

A retelling from the original story
by the Brothers Grimm

There was a time when everyone
believed in elves. The shoemaker and
his wife in this story certainly did!

The shoemaker worked hard from
morning to night. The shoes he made were
of the finest leather, but business was slow.
One night he found he only had enough
leather left for one more pair of shoes. He
cut the leather carefully and left the pieces
ready on his work bench to sew the next
morning. Then he crossed the yard from his

little shop into the house.

"Wife, I do not know what we shall do. I have just cut out the last piece of leather in the shop," he said sadly.

"Don't be too gloomy," said his wife. "Perhaps you will be able to sell this last pair of shoes for a fine price."

The next day the shoemaker was up early as usual. When he pulled back the shutters in the shop, he saw not pieces of leather ready to sew on the bench, but a fine pair of ladies' shoes with delicate pointed toes. The stitching was so fine you would think it had been done by mice. He put the shoes in the window of the shop, and before long a rich merchant came in and bought the shoes for his wife, paying the shoemaker double the usual price. The shoemaker was delighted, and bought enough leather to make two new pairs of shoes. Once again, he cut the leather, and left the pieces on his work bench to sew the next day.

The next mornig the shoemaker was up earlier than usual. His wife came with him as he went into the shop, and pulled back the shutters.

"Oh husband," she gasped, for there on the bench stood two pairs of the finest shoes she had ever seen. There was a green pair with red heels, and a pair so shiny and black the shoemaker could see his face in them. He put the shoes in the window, and very quickly in came a poet who bought the green pair, and not far behind him there was a parson who bought the black pair. Both paid him a great deal of money for the splendid shoes.

This continued for many days. The shoemaker would buy new leather and

leave the pieces cut ready on his bench at night, and when he came back in the morning there would be the most exquisite shoes. The shoemaker's reputation spread, and his shop was soon full of customers. Before long the shoemaker and his wife were no longer poor.

One day, the wife said, "Husband, I think we must see who it is who has given us this great good fortune so we may thank them."

The shoemaker agreed, so that night after laying out the cut leather pieces, he and his wife hid behind the door of the shop. As the town hall clock struck midnight, they heard a scampering of tiny feet and little voices.

Two elves slid out from behind the skirting
board and climbed onto the bench where
they were soon hard at work. The elves sang
as they stitched, but they looked poor. Their
trousers were ragged, their shirts were
threadbare and their feet looked frozen
as they had neither
socks nor shoes.

Soon the leather was gone and on the
bench stood more shoes. The elves slipped
away.

The next day, the shoemaker took some
green and yellow leather and made two
little pairs of boots, yellow with green heels.

The wife took some cloth and made two little pairs of red trousers and two green jackets. She also knitted two pairs of socks. That night, they laid out the clothes and boots, and hid behind the shop door.

As the town hall clock struck midnight, the two elves slid out from behind the skirting board and climbed onto the bench. When they saw the gifts, they clapped their hands in delight, flung off their old rags and tried on their new clothes and boots. They looked splendid. Then they slipped behind the skirting board, and the shoemaker and his wife never saw them again.

But once a year when the shoemaker opened the shop in the morning, on his bench he would find a pair of shoes with stitching so fine you would think it had been done by mice.

Little Miss Muffet

Little Miss Muffet
Sat on a tuffet,
Eating her curds and whey.

There came a big spider,
Who sat down beside her,
And frightened Miss Muffet away.

There was a Crooked Man

There was a crooked man,
And he walked a crooked mile,
He found a crooked sixpence
Against a crooked stile,

He bought a crooked cat,
Which caught a crooked mouse,
And they all lived together
In a little crooked house.

I had a Little Nut Tree

I had a little nut tree,
Nothing would it bear
But a silver nutmeg and a golden pear;
The King of Spain's daughter
Came to visit me,
And all for the sake
Of my little nut tree.

The Frog Prince

A retelling from the original story
by the Brothers Grimm

Once upon a time, there lived a very spoilt princess who never seemed content. The more she had, the more she wanted. And she just would not do as she was told.

One day she took her golden ball out into the woods, although she had been told by her chief nanny that she must embroider some new handkerchiefs. She threw the golden ball high up into the sky once, twice, but the third time it slipped from her hands and, with a great splash, it fell down, down into a deep well. The princess stamped her foot and yelled, but this did not help. So she kicked the side of the well, and was just getting ready for another big yell, when a very large frog plopped out of the well.

"Ugh!" said the princess. "A horrible slimy frog," but the frog didn't move. Instead, it said, "What are you making such a fuss about?"

A talking frog! For a moment the princess was speechless, but then she looked down her nose and said, "If you must know, my golden ball has fallen down this well, and I want it back."

With a sudden leap, the frog disappeared down the well. In the wink of an eye, it was back with the golden ball.

The princess went to snatch it up, but the frog put a wet foot rather firmly on it and said, "Hasn't anyone taught you any manners? 'Please' and 'thank you' would not go amiss, and anyway I have a special request to make."

The princess looked at the frog in utter astonishment. No one ever dared talk to her like that, and certainly not a frog. She glared at the frog and said crossly, "May I have my ball back, please, and what is your special request?"

The frog did not move its foot, but bent closer to the princess.

"I want to come and live with you in the palace and eat off your plate and sleep on your pillow, please."

The princess looked horrified, but she was sure a promise to a frog wouldn't count so she said, "Of course," and grabbed her ball from frog and ran back to the palace.

That night at supper the royal family heard a strange voice calling, "Princess, where are you?" and in hopped the frog.

The queen fainted. The king frowned.

"Do you know this frog?" he asked.

"Oh bother!" said the princess, but she had to tell her father what had happened. When he heard the story, he insisted the princess keep her promise.

The frog ate very little, the princess even less. And when it was time to go to bed, the king just looked very sternly at the princess who was trying to sneak off on her own. She bent down and picked the frog up by one leg, and when she reached her great four-poster bed, she plonked the frog down in the farthest corner. She did not sleep a wink all night.

The next evening, the frog was back. Supper was a quiet affair. The queen stayed

in her room, the king read the newspaper, and the princess tried not to look at the frog. Bedtime came, and once again the frog and the princess slept at opposite ends of the bed.

The third evening, the princess was terribly hungry so she just pretended the frog was not there and ate everything that was placed in front of her. When it came to bedtime, she was so exhausted that she fell in a deep sleep as soon as her head touched the pillow.

The next morning when she woke up, she felt much better for her good sleep until she remembered the frog. But it was nowhere to be seen. At the foot of the bed, however, there stood a handsome young man in a green velvet suit.

"Hello, princess. Do you know that you snore?" he said.

The princess's mouth fell open ready to
yell, but the handsome young man said,
"I don't suppose you recognize me, thank
goodness, but I was the frog who rescued
your golden ball. I was bewitched by a fairy
who said I was rude and spoilt," and here
the young man looked sideways at the
princess whose mouth was still hanging
open, "And the spell could only be broken

by someone equally rude and spoilt having to be nice to me."

The princess closed her mouth. The king was most impressed with the young man's good manners, and the queen liked the look of his fine green velvet suit. Everyone liked the fact that the princess had become a much nicer person. Before long it seemed sensible for the princess and the handsome young man to get married. They had lots of children who were not at all spoilt and everyone lived happily ever after. The golden ball and the green velvet suit were put away in a very dark cupboard.

Pop goes the Weasel

Half a pound of tuppenny rice,
Half a pound of treacle,
That's the way the money goes,
Pop goes the weasel!

Up and down the City Road,
In and out The Eagle,
That's the way the money goes,
Pop goes the weasel!

Every night when I go out
The monkey's on the table,
Take a stick and knock it off,
Pop goes the weasel!

The Muffin Man

Do you know the muffin man,
The muffin man, the muffin man,
Do you know the muffin man,
Who lives in Drury Lane?

Yes, I know the muffin man,
The muffin man, the muffin man,
Yes, I know the muffin man,
Who lives in Drury Lane.

Chicken Licken

An English folk tale

One fine day Chicken Licken went for a walk in the woods. Now Chicken Licken was not very bright, and he was also rather inclined to act first and think after. So when an acorn fell on his head, he decided immediately that the sky must be falling in. He set off as fast as he could to tell the king. On the way he met Henny Penny and Cocky Locky.

"I am off to tell the king that the sky is falling in," he clucked importantly.

"We will come too," said Henny Penny and Cocky Locky.

So Chicken Licken, Henny Penny and Cocky Locky set off to find the King. On the way they met Ducky Lucky and Drakey Lakey.

"We are off to tell the king that the sky is falling in," clucked Chicken Licken importantly.

"We will come too," said Ducky Lucky and Drakey Lakey.

So Chicken Licken, Henny Penny, Cocky Locky, Ducky Lucky and Drakey Lakey all set off to find the king. On the way they met Goosey Loosey and Turkey Lurkey.

"We are off to tell the king that the sky is falling in," clucked Chicken Licken importantly.

"We will come too," said Goosey Loosey and Turkey Lurkey.

So Chicken Licken, Henny Penny, Cocky Locky, Ducky Lucky, Drakey Lakey, Goosey Loosey and Turkey Lurkey all set off to find the king. On the way they met Foxy Loxy.

"We are off to tell the king that the sky is falling in," clucked Chicken Licken importantly.

"What a good thing I met you all," said

Foxy Loxy with a cunning smile. "I know the way, follow me."

So Chicken Licken, Henny Penny, Cocky Locky, Ducky Lucky, Drakey Lakey, Goosey Loosey and Turkey Lurkey all set off behind Foxy Loxy. He led them all straight to his den where he ate every single one of them for his dinner! So the king never heard that the sky was falling in. (It didn't, of course.)

I Saw Three Ships

I saw three ships come sailing by,
Come sailing by, come sailing by,
I saw three ships come sailing by,
On New Year's Day in the morning.

And what do you think was in them then,
Was in them then, was in them then?
And what do you think was in them then,
On New Year's Day in the morning?

Three pretty girls were in them then,
Were in them then, were in them then,
Three pretty girls were in them then,
On New Year's Day in the morning.

What are Little Boys made of?

What are little boys made of?
What are little boys made of?
Frogs and snails and puppy-dogs' tails,
That's what little boys are made of.

What are little girls made of?
What are little girls made of?
Sugar and spice and all things nice,
That's what little girls are made of.

How many Miles to Babylon?

How many Miles
to Babylon?
Three score and ten.
Can I get there
by candlelight?
Aye, and back again.
If your feet are
nimble and light,
You'll get there
by candlelight.